empty

zilch

bupkus

zero

null

NOTHING

nought

DISCARD

zot

Void

nothing

diddly squat

zippo

zip

goose egg

nothing

scratch

nothing

nil

nada

blank

mike bender

illustrated by hugh murphy

THE BOOK ABOUT
NOTHING

CROWN BOOKS FOR YOUNG READERS  New York

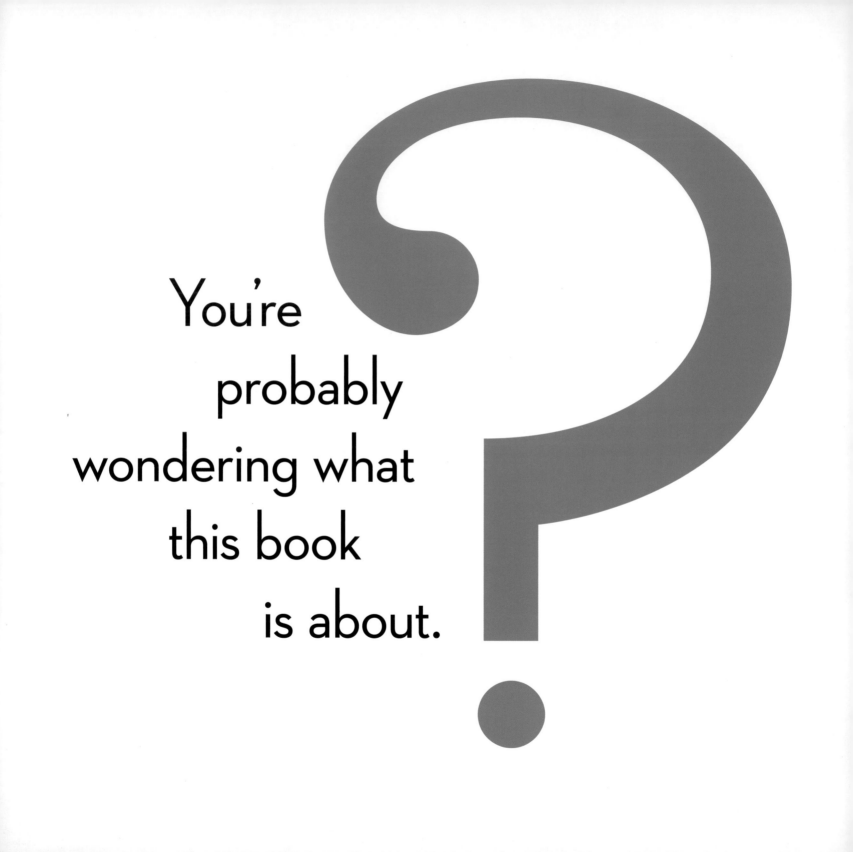

You're probably wondering what this book is about.

Before we get to that,
here are a few things it **WON'T** be about. . . .

Rainbows, clouds, stars, the sun, the moon, rocket ships, planes, helicopters, diggers, cars, taxis, buses, sailboats, tugboats, canoes, submarines, crayons, flowers, socks, meatballs, blueberries, tacos, ice cream, lollipops, doctors, firefighters, farmers, kings, queens, princes, princesses.

And no, this book will definitely NOT be about UNDERPANTS.

Sorry, underpants fans.

So
then what **is**
this book about

I'll

give

you

a

clue.

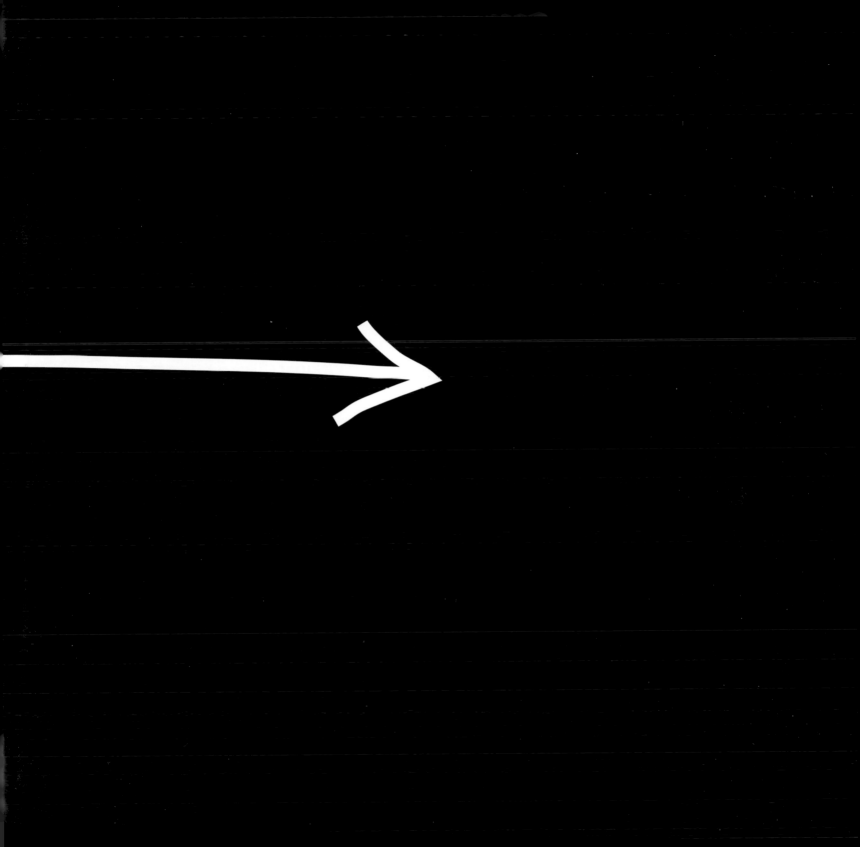

Haven't guessed it yet?

This book is about nothing!

That's right.

NOTHING.

But how can a book be about *nothing*?

Well, because . . .

are you ready for this?

Even nothing is

something.

Take this cookie jar. If you eat all the
chocolate chip cookies, the jar will be empty. Right?

Wrong. It will be chock-full of

nothing.

If you pick up all the toys in your room,
there will be **nothing** on the floor
(and that will make your parents happy).

If you eat everything on this plate,

there will be **nothing left**

(and that will make your parents *very* happy).

When you go poop and flush,
guess what's left in there.

Oh, no.
You forgot to flush!

Ahem. As I was saying . . .

nothing.

When you take a bath,

guess what you're wearing.

Nothing.

You can clean your teeth
with **nothing** on the brush.

Of course, then your teeth will fall out
and there will be **nothing** in your mouth.

At night,

when you shut off the lights to go to bed,

what can you see?

NOTHING!

CREEEEEEEEEEEE-AAAAAAAAAKKKKK!

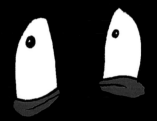

(And by the way, if you hear a strange noise in the middle of the night, go back to sleep—it's just good ol' nothin'.)

With nothing, **anything** is possible.

You can run with **nothing** on your feet.

You can trip over nothing.

You might accidentally burp in someone's face.

Then when they ask, "What was that?" you can say,

"Oh, nothing."

You can get a bunch of balloons

and a big cake and celebrate

And you can even sit and
do nothing.

(Which really hits the spot

after a long day of doing everything!)

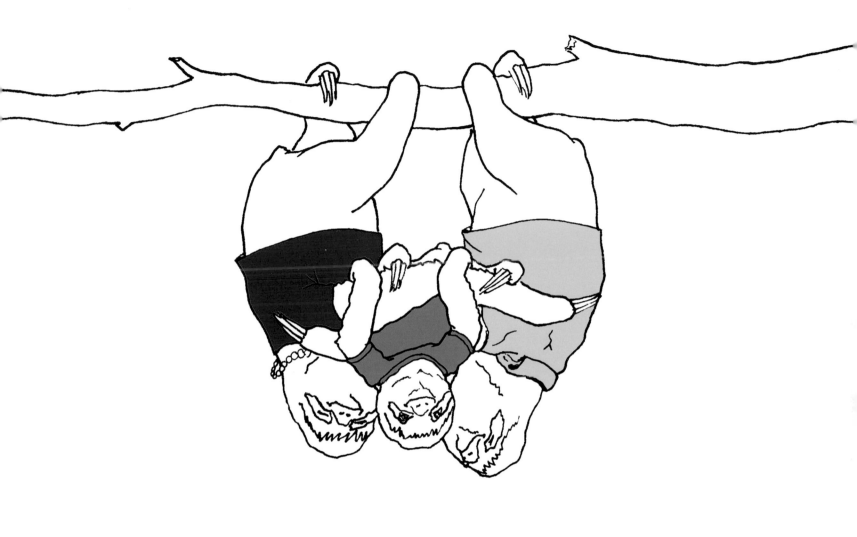

But best of all is a hug from your parents,
because it feels great and costs
absolutely nothing.

So now that you've read this book,

I hope you've learned

one very important thing. . . .

You're going to make me say it again, aren't you?

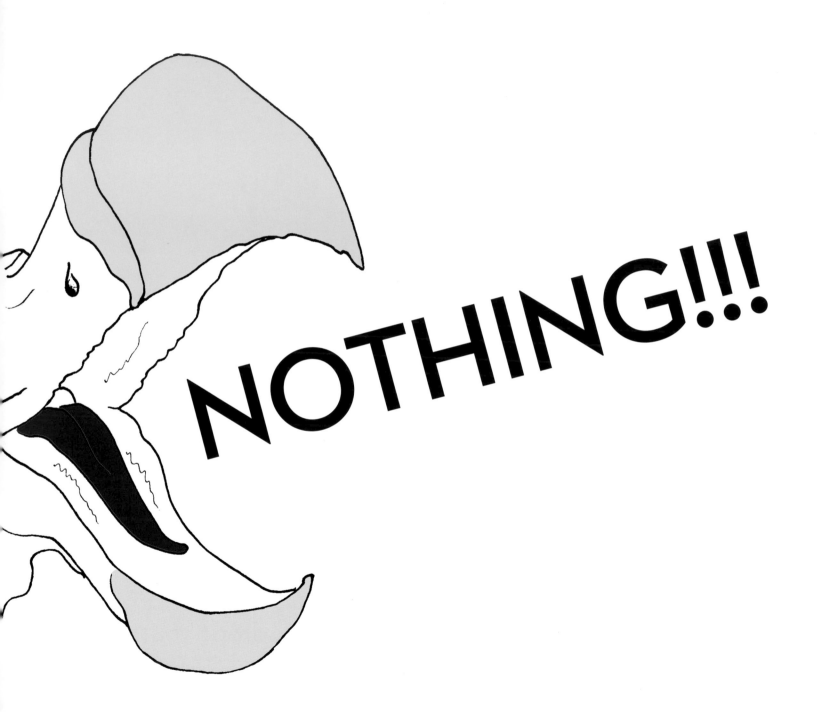

For Kai and Soe
"Don't underestimate the value of doing nothing."—Winnie-the-Pooh
—M.B.

For my girls, Sarah and Sloane
—H.M.

All rights reserved. Published in the United States by Crown Books for Young Readers,
an imprint of Random House Children's Books, a division of Penguin Random House LLC, New York.

Crown and the colophon are registered trademarks of Penguin Random House LLC.

Visit us on the Web! randomhousekids.com

Educators and librarians, for a variety of teaching tools, visit us at RHTeachersLibrarians.com

Library of Congress Cataloging-in-Publication Data is available upon request.
ISBN 978-0-399-55109-3 (trade) — ISBN 978-0-399-55110-9 (lib. bdg.) — ISBN 978-0-399-55111-6 (ebook)

MANUFACTURED IN CHINA
10 9 8 7 6 5 4 3 2 1
First Edition

nothing

nada

zip

oddiz.

zero

bupkus

empty

null

zilch

nil.

NOTHING

goose egg

zot

nought

scratch

void

blank

nothing

diddly squat

nothing